THE ADVENTURES OF PIRATE BILL

Barbara Williams-Carr

Illustrated by
Andrew Roper
www.worldofroper.com

ARTHUR H. STOCKWELL LTD
Torrs Park   Ilfracombe   Devon
Established 1898
www.ahstockwell.co.uk

British Library Cataloguing-in-Publication Data.
A catalogue record for this book is available
from the British Library.

ISBN 978-0-7223-4112-4
Printed in Great Britain by
Arthur H. Stockwell Ltd
Torrs Park   Ilfracombe
Devon

PIRATE BILL AND THE FROG PRINCE

Pirate Bill lived in Trawley Bay, a sleepy little village in a faraway land, just down the coast from Dreamy Cove. Pirate Bill was not married; he lived in his little two-bedroomed cottage with his little dog, Sprite.

Sprite was a very lively terrier pup who was always looking for adventure. Sprite loved going out on the boat with Pirate Bill.

One misty morning in October, Bill took his boat out to look for treasure. Bill had found an old map while digging in his vegetable patch the day before, and an X on the map indicated a cave just around the headland in Dreamy Cove.

"Come on, lad – let's go find us some treasure," Bill said to Sprite.

Sprite was raring to go – he loved adventures. Bill's 'adventures' rarely led to anything, but Sprite loved being out with his master anyway. Sprite licked Bill's hand, and off they went down to the harbour.

Bill's boat stood out from everyone else's. It did look a very odd vessel. There was a skull and crossbones on the sail, a dragon's head at the front, two windows in the side and a drawbridge in the middle. The drawbridge did not work – it was only for show – but Bill thought it looked good.

As you may have guessed, Bill was not a real pirate. He just liked to pretend. Everyone in Trawley Bay thought Bill was a little strange, but everyone liked him – especially the boys and girls, because Bill told them stories about all his adventures on the sea in his boat, the *Punky Dragon*.

Little Pike Trout swore that when he grew up (he was only five) he would go out with Bill on his boat; and his dad, Roach Trout, said that when Pike was tall enough to touch his beard he would let him go. Unfortunately, Pike was unaware that his father intended to shave his beard off as soon as Pike was tall enough to touch it.

Bill and Sprite boarded the *Punky Dragon* and set sail for Dreamy Cove. Bill told Sprite that he had a good feeling about this adventure, and he said he would buy Sprite a steak dinner when they returned with their treasure.

Sprite woofed his delight and wagged his tail vigorously, thinking, 'That sounds delicious, but I don't really mind if I only have leftovers from my master's plate.'

As Bill and Sprite rounded Dreamy Cove in the *Punky Dragon*, the mist started to thicken. Bill swore he heard a croaking noise coming from the rocks. Sprite heard it too. He got very excited and started running up and down the *Punky Dragon*. Bill was looking very hard through his spyglass (which he had borrowed years ago from the Cariba Creek Public House on the corner of the road where he lived, Crab Street).

Bill suddenly shouted, "Hi, Sprity boy, I can see an entrance to a cave on the starboard side."

Sprite ran to the starboard side, only to realise that Pirate Bill was standing looking out over the port side. Bill had never quite got the hang of port and starboard. Sprite let out a sigh and joined Bill on the port side just as they swung round into the entrance of a very small cave.

As the *Punky Dragon* entered the cave, Bill and Sprite could hear the strange croaking sound again. They both looked at each other in amazement. The sound echoed around the cave. It sounded like a million frogs croaking all at once. Bill manoeuvred the *Punky Dragon* into the cave and jumped off the boat on to a rock to find some way of tying the boat up.

Left on the boat by himself, Sprite thought he heard a noise from below. He had just started to go down the first step when he heard Bill coming back, so he excitedly ran back up on deck, forgetting all about the noise below.

Bill had tied the *Punky Dragon* up to a small rock. Sprite jumped off the boat and ran around excitedly. As Sprite ran over to his master, who had just been to collect his pick and shovel from the *Punky Dragon*, the little dog could have sworn he saw a face at the window of the boat.

Sprite stood staring, then started to bark, and he ran back to the *Punky Dragon*, but Bill was heading towards the back of the cave, shouting, "Come on, lad – keep up."

Sprite ran after his master, not wanting to miss out on the adventure of finding any treasure. Deep inside the cave, Bill and Sprite could still hear the strange croaking sound, but it was now fainter. Sprite ran ahead of Bill, very excited, even deeper into the cave. Sprite stopped. He was sure he saw a shadow behind him on the cave wall.

Just as Sprite turned to go back to take a look, Bill shouted, "Hey, lad, there's a light up ahead. Come on – what is the matter with you today? Don't you want to find the treasure?"

Sprite, not wanting to upset his master, turned back and ran after him. As they went deeper into the cave the light became brighter.

"Oh, lad, I'm not too sure about this. Maybe we should go back."

Sprite barked excitedly and ran forward, turning to look at Bill.

"Oh, go on, then," Bill said nervously. (Bill was not really very brave, but he did not want to upset Sprite.)

The light glowed very brightly from a small hole in the depths of the cave, and Sprite very nervously crawled on his tummy towards the hole.

"Be careful, lad," whispered Bill, standing back with his shovel raised above his head.

Sprite looked into the hole and something jumped up. Sprite yelped and ran to hide behind Bill. As he did this, both Bill and Sprite heard a squeal behind them. They both turned at the same time to see little Pike Trout running towards them. Bill and Sprite looked at each other in amazement. Pike flung his arms around Bill and started to shake. All three were huddled together.

Bill was asking Pike how on earth he had got there when they heard a small croaking voice: "Help me! Please help me get out of this hole."

All three turned to look into the hole, and they saw a big green frog crying. Bill bent over to take a closer look, and Pike was hanging on nervously to his trousers. Bill shook his head in disbelief. A talking, crying frog! Never!

The frog spoke again, this time in a calmer voice: "Could you please help me? I have been stuck down this hole for such a long time and I cannot jump high enough to get out."

Bill then managed to find his voice. "Why are you down there?" he asked. "If we help you, will you promise not to harm us in any way?"

The frog explained that his name was Prince Solaro and he had been left in the hole in the cave by a wizard who was working for his uncle and wanted him out of the way so that he could run his kingdom. He told Bill that if he helped him he would make him rich.

Bill was not sure whether he believed the frog. He could not help but worry about Pike; if anything happened to him, his poor parents would be so upset. So Bill decided to take Pike back to the *Punky Dragon* first, and he told Sprite to stay with him to protect him.

After making sure that Pike and Sprite were safely below deck on the *Punky Dragon*, Bill asked the frog how he could be sure he could trust him.

The frog said that if he could just get to water he would prove who he was.

Bill put his shovel as far as he could reach down the hole and told the frog to jump on to it. The frog jumped as high as he could and managed to scramble on to Bill's shovel. As Bill lifted his shovel out of the hole, the frog gave a mighty leap on to the rocks, and, with Bill running after him, the frog made another mighty leap into the sea.

Pike and Sprite were looking out of one of the *Punky Dragon*'s windows, and they saw the frog disappear into the sea with a splash. Bill had just made up his mind to return to the *Punky Dragon* when a man rose up from the water, coughing and spluttering.

"It must have been true, then," said Bill.

After he had helped the Prince on board, Bill found him some old clothes and they had a drink and some sandwiches which Bill had packed for himself and Sprite.

The Prince was very grateful, and he asked Bill if he could drop him off on one of the islands just off Trawley Bay; from there he could make his way back to his own country on a cargo ship.

Bill chatted to the Prince on their way to Puffin Island, where Bill knew there would be regular cargo ships docking. Bill also chatted to little Pike Trout to find out how he had come to be on the *Punky Dragon*.

Pike said he had waited until his father had left for work, and then he had sneaked on to the *Punky Dragon* and hidden in a barrel. Pike said he had heard Bill telling Sprite about going on an adventure, and he had wanted to go too; he knew that he would not be given permission because he could not touch his father's beard yet. Bill asked him what he meant by that, and Pike explained. Bill laughed and so did Prince Solaro; Sprite woofed and wagged his tail.

Bill dropped the Prince off at Puffin Island, and the Prince promised to be in touch soon.

Then Bill said, "We had better get you back home, little Pike Trout, before your parents get really worried."

Pike said, "What shall I tell them, Bill? They will want to know where I have been."

Bill said, "You should always tell the truth, little Pike," but Bill knew full well that his parents would not believe him.

As the *Punky Dragon* pulled into the harbour at Trawley Bay everyone was just returning from work – including Pike's father – so Bill waited until they had all left the harbour before taking Pike home. When they arrived, Mr and Mrs Trout were outside looking for him. Pike often spent time with Bill at his cottage, so his parents weren't worried when they saw them coming up the path together. Bill picked little Pike up so that the boy could touch his father's beard; then Bill and little Pike winked at each other and Sprite yapped and wagged his tail. They knew what they knew, but they weren't letting on to anyone.

Bill handed little Pike to his father and turned to walk back down the path to his own little cottage with Sprite hot on his heels.

What a good adventure Bill, Sprite and Pike had!

Are you laughing as loud as Mr and Mrs Trout did when Pike told them this story? Could it really be true?